Dear Parent:
Your child's love of reading starts here!

Every child learns to read in a different way and at his or her own speed. Some go back and forth between reading levels and read favorite books again and again. Others read through each level in order. You can help your young reader improve and become more confident by encouraging his or her own interests and abilities. From books your child reads with you to the first books he or she reads alone, there are I Can Read Books for every stage of reading:

SHARED READING
Basic language, word repetition, and whimsical illustrations, ideal for sharing with your emergent reader

BEGINNING READING
Short sentences, familiar words, and simple concepts for children eager to read on their own

READING WITH HELP
Engaging stories, longer sentences, and language play for developing readers

READING ALONE
Complex plots, challenging vocabulary, and high-interest topics for the independent reader

ADVANCED READING
Short paragraphs, chapters, and exciting themes for the perfect bridge to chapter books

I Can Read Books have introduced children to the joy of reading since 1957. Featuring award-winning authors and illustrators and a fabulous cast of beloved characters, I Can Read Books set the standard for beginning readers.

A lifetime of discovery begins with the magical words **"I Can Read!"**

Visit www.icanread.com for information on enriching your child's reading experience.

For Aslang Nodset
—J.L.N.

For Steven, Susan, and Jasper
—P.M.

HarperCollins®, ☘®, and I Can Read Book® are trademarks of HarperCollins Publishers.

Library of Congress Cataloging-in-Publication Data

Lexau, Joan M.
  Go away, dog / story by Joan L. Nodset ; pictures by Paul Meisel.
    p. cm.—(A my first I can read book)
  Summary: An old dog's friendly persistence slowly convinces a young boy to take him home.
  ISBN-10: 0-06-444231-4 (pbk.) — ISBN-13: 978-0-06-444231-2 (pbk.)
  [1. Dogs—Fiction.] I. Meisel, Paul, ill. II. Title. III. Series.
PZ7.L5895Go 1997   96-27272
[E]—dc20   CIP
                                              AC

❖
10 11 12 13 SCP 30 29 28 27

I Can Read!

SHARED My First READING

Go Away, Dog

STORY BY JOAN L. NODSET
PICTURES BY PAUL MEISEL

HarperCollinsPublishers

Go away, you bad old dog.

Go away from me.

I don't like you, dog.
I don't like dogs at all.

Big dogs, little dogs.

Any dogs at all.

I don't want that stick.
Don't give it to me.

If I throw the stick,
will you go away?

10

There now, go away
with your stick.

What do you want now?
If I throw it again,
will you go away?

Don't jump on me, dog.

I don't like that.

Go away, you old dog.

Go on home now.

Don't you have a home?
Well, that is too bad.

But you cannot

come home with me.

Don't wag your tail at me.

I don't like dogs.

You are not bad for a dog.

But I don't like dogs.

Say, do that again.

Roll over again, dog.

Say, that is not bad.

Can you shake hands?

This is how

to shake hands.

Don't lick my hand.

Stop that, you old dog.

If I play with you,
will you go away?

All right, let's run, dog.

Can you run
as fast as I can?

You can run fast all right.

That was fun, dog.

Maybe we can play again.

But I have to go home now.

No, you cannot come.

Go away now, dog.

Don't look so sad, dog.

Don't lick my hand.
Can I help it
if you don't have a home?

Why don't you go away?
You like me, don't you,
you old dog?

Well, I like you, too.
All right, I give up.

Come on home, dog.
Come on, let's run.